The
Bible Time Travelers

Book One: *A Giant Problem*

KARLY CROSS

LifeRich Publishing is a registered trademark of The Reader's Digest Association, Inc.

LifeRich Publishing books may be ordered through booksellers or by contacting:

LifeRich Publishing
1663 Liberty Drive
Bloomington, IN 47403
www.liferichpublishing.com
844-686-9607

Because of the dynamic nature of the Internet, any web addresses or links contained in this book may have changed since publication and may no longer be valid. The views expressed in this work are solely those of the author and do not necessarily reflect the views of the publisher, and the publisher hereby disclaims any responsibility for them.

This is a work of fiction. All of the characters, names, incidents, organizations, and dialogue in this novel are either the products of the author's imagination or are used fictitiously.

Any people depicted in stock imagery provided by Getty Images are models, and such images are being used for illustrative purposes only. Certain stock imagery © Getty Images.

ISBN: 978-1-4897-3121-0 (sc)
ISBN: 978-1-4897-3138-8 (e)

Library of Congress Control Number: 2020919666

Print information available on the last page.

LifeRich Publishing rev. date: 10/08/2020

Dedicated to Evelyn Ruth. May you
always stay curious and love God.

ONE

Riley Carson sat on her front stoop, anxious for her parents' blue van to pull around the corner and into the driveway. Today was the day that her father was coming home from his first trip with Biblical Expeditions, a company with a mission to find items from the time of the Bible. She had heard her dad saying to her mom that this was a trip of a lifetime. He had apparently been trying to get on with Biblical Expeditions for months, and now his time had finally come. He had only been gone for four weeks, but to Riley, it felt like forever.

Riley's mom had left to go pick him up from the airport about an hour before his flight arrived. Riley's older sister, Reese, stayed home to babysit, "because ten is still too young to be by yourself." Riley wanted to play soccer with her, but she was inside talking on the phone with her gross boyfriend, Stone. *Teenagers are weird*, thought Riley as she heard Reese giggle from her open bedroom window. *I'm never getting a boyfriend!*

"Could you keep it down a little?" Riley yelled up at her sister.

"Leave me alone, Riley!" Reese shouted back as she popped her head out the window and stuck her tongue out at her sister.

Sisters are the worst, Riley concluded in her mind.

She was very eager for her parents to get home. Her foot started tapping the ground, and she began to mess with her hair. Riley looked over at the sound of footsteps and saw her best friend and next-door neighbor, Gabe Donovan, walking up to her. "Is your dad home yet?" he asked.

"No," she said. "He should definitely be home by now."

"Well I know what will distract you," Gabe said, stealing the soccer ball from her side. "Betcha I can score a goal on you before you can me." He pointed to trees on either side of the yard as goalposts.

"But I can't win." Riley sighed. "You're stronger and faster than me. I'd lose in an instant."

"That's the point," Gabe said, laughing, "I'm challenging you because I know I'll win." Riley made a *hmph* noise and crossed her arms. It wasn't fair. Riley couldn't help that she wasn't as good as him, but he still liked to pick on her. As Gabe laughed, the Carson family van parked in the driveway.

"He's here!" Riley launched from the steps and ran to the car. As soon as her dad stepped out of the car, she jumped into his arms.

"Hey, sweet girl," he said, his scruffy beard tickling her shoulder.

Riley pulled away and looked at her father. "You're so tan!"

"I know! The sun is ten times hotter in Israel than it is here!" Her dad lifted a hand up toward Reese's window, where she was waving. "And I have so much to tell you," he continued. "But let's talk about it over dinner. We stopped and picked up pizza on the way home."

Mrs. Carson was carrying the pizza in the door when she passed by Gabe. "Gabe," she said, "you are welcome to stay for dinner, too! I know you are excited to hear Mr. Carson's stories."

"Sure, Mrs. Carson!" Gabe's brown eyes lit up with excitement. He ran into the house, leaving the soccer ball behind in the yard. Mr. Carson and Riley pulled his suitcases out of the trunk.

"Was that boy picking on you, Riley?" asked her dad.

"Kind of," she said, "but it's okay. He just likes to tease me because he's better at soccer."

"You know," said Mr. Carson, "a little faith can go a long way in being a better player, no matter the game."

Riley shrugged. "If you say so, Dad. But I don't think it'll work in this case."

Mr. Carson laughed. "One day you'll see," he said. "I promise."

TWO

"So," said Riley's dad as the Carsons and Gabe settled in to eat, "we went to this place called the Valley of Elah. It's near Bethlehem over in Israel. And let me tell you, it's hotter than our worst Ohio summer!"

"Reese," interjected Mrs. Carson, "no phones at the table, please. Stone can wait."

Reese rolled her eyes, then put her phone down and turned her attention to her dad.

"The Valley of Elah," Mr. Carson continued, "is the place where David fought Goliath. And we think we know its present-day location."

"Like we learned in Bible class?" Riley asked, eyes wide with wonder. Even Reese looked impressed.

"*Exactly* like you learned in Bible class," replied Mr. Carson.

"So, was it actually, you know, the real deal?" asked Gabe, his mouth full of pizza.

"Well," said Mr. Carson, "we dug for about three weeks and found nothing. Just more and more dirt. But then," he said, reaching behind him into his backpack, "we found *this*." He pulled out a black box, and inside was an object wrapped in a thin brown cloth. When he opened the cloth, there lay an old, leather slingshot with thin straps.

"Whoa." Riley and Gabe said this in unison.

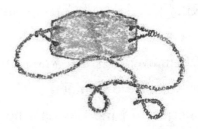

"What if a tourist just had that there?" asked Reese. "Or it was, like, from another time or something? Not Bible times."

"Well, that's why I have it here." Mr. Carson carefully put the slingshot back in its wrapping and box. "See, Biblical Expeditions asked me to take it to an artifact specialist in Cleveland tomorrow to see if we can date it more accurately. But I and several others on our team think it might be, as you kids say, legit."

"Whoa," Riley and Gabe said together again.

"I hope it *is* real," said Riley, "that way the world has something that awesome."

"Me too," said Gabe, "but because that would make it the coolest weapon of all time!"

Mrs. Carson laughed, picking up everybody's empty plates. "Now, you two go wash your greasy hands and play a little bit before it gets dark. You need to get all that energy out."

Reese, instead of going to play, too, ran back up to her room to continue the phone call with her boyfriend.

Riley and Gabe made their way back outside and sat down on the front step. "Do you think," asked Gabe, "that *that* slingshot killed a giant? It seems a bit impossible to me."

"Well, I don't know. But if it's the real one, then the Bible says it did. And the Bible tells the truth."

Gabe shook his head, messing up his hair in the process. "Nah, nothing that little can defeat a big old giant."

"Hey," Riley whispered, scooting closer to Gabe, "if we wait a little bit, we can probably sneak into my dad's office and get a closer look. That's where he always keeps important things."

Gabe nodded quickly, smiling in excitement. "I am *so* in. Let's do it."

They kicked the soccer ball around for a while, Gabe scoring on Riley every time and Riley caring about the game less and less. After Gabe had scored his tenth goal, they sneaked inside.

The late summer sun was starting to set. Riley's parents were on the couch watching some sort of comedy show, and Reese was still talking to Stone, and the two friends knew that this was their chance. Riley and Gabe tiptoed carefully down the hallway all the way to Mr. Carson's office. Riley slowly turned the knob, and she and Gabe entered the room.

The walls were lined with what seemed like hundreds of books about history and time. There were empty display cases all around, waiting for Riley's dad to fill them up with other lost treasures. In the middle of the room was her dad's big brown desk, complete with a lamp and laptop. Next to his laptop, though, was what they were really looking for: the black box.

Riley opened the box carefully and peeled back the smooth brown cloth to reveal the slingshot. It looked more worn down and beat-up when they were closer to it, but it still made them feel excited to be that close.

"I don't know if we should touch it," whispered Riley, "Dad acted like it was too precious to touch. Like the china Mom has in the high cabinets."

"Oh, don't be such a sissy," Gabe hissed back, and before Riley could stop him, he took hold of the slingshot. That's when the world began to flash.

Riley put her hand on top of Gabe's, which was holding the slingshot tightly. "What's happening?" Riley covered her eyes from the brightness while what sounded like a roar rang in their ears.

"I don't know," Gabe shouted. "Just hold on!" The air around them began to rush, making their hair fly all around them. The lights got brighter, the roar got louder, the wind got faster, and then, just as quickly as it started, it stopped.

THREE

For a moment, Riley just stood there, her hand over her eyes. Her skin was starting to feel warm, and it felt like her shoes had flown off in the rush. She heard Gabe gasp next to her, and that's when she uncovered her eyes. They definitely were *not* in her father's office anymore.

All around them were small hills and grassy fields. The sun was shining like it was morning and there were short but wide trees scattered around them. Birds were singing above them and below them was a dirt path.

"Gabe," said Riley, "our clothes."

Gabe looked down like Riley was and, to both of their surprise, they weren't in their tee-shirts and sneakers anymore, but in rough tunics that went down just past their knees and thin sandals. Gabe tugged at the blue fabric with his free hand. "Aw great, a skirt?!"

Riley giggled at how Gabe was reacting and then her eyes widened in horror. "Gabe," she said shakily, "where's the slingshot?"

Gabe froze in the place, and looked at his hands...the slingshot was gone! However, in its place, wrapped in Gabe's clenched fist was a small, crumpled note.

"Open it," encouraged Riley, "and make it fast."

Gabe opened the note and read it out loud. "The one who delivers must deliver the slingshot to you."

"Weird," said Gabe. He scrunched up his face in confusion. *How is this all happening?* He thought. *Is this all a dream?* He turned to Riley. "Pinch me," he said. She reached out a small hand and pinched his arm tightly. "OUCH! Not so hard!" He shook his head. "Well, we can rule out this being a dream."

Riley's face quickly turned worried. "What do we do? Where even are we?"

"Definitely not Ohio," laughed Gabe uncomfortably.

Riley looked around for any indication of where they were, and that's when she spotted a wooden signpost a few yards away. "This way!" She ran towards the signpost, Gabe eventually passing her and making it there first. In one direction pointed an arrow that said "Bethlehem" and on another pointing the opposite way said the word "Gath."

"Bethlehem..." said Gabe, "isn't that where your dad just was?"

"Yeah," said Riley, "but that's impossible, right? How can we be all the way over there?"

"Well, we already know it's not a dream," whispered Gabe. Reality sunk in. This was real life. "And, Riley," he said, "since it's *not* a dream, then we have to ask another important question. We know *where* we are...but do we know *when* we are? Because these weird dresses are *not* for sale back home."

Before Riley could answer, a low growl came from somewhere near her. She looked at Gabe and laughed. "You had, like, 4 slices of pizza," she said, "there's no way you're still hungry." She stopped laughing when she saw the look of fear on her friend's face.

"Riley," Gabe said, his voice cracking, "that wasn't my stomach."

The two friends turned around slowly, goosebumps creeping over their arms. There, lying in the grass, crouched down, was a big, ferocious, lion. Its tail was rigid and its shoulders rolled as it stalked the two kids.

"Gabe," said Riley, both of them slowly walking back as the lion crept forward, "what do we do?"

Gabe didn't answer. His mouth was open, but no words were coming out. The lion bared its teeth and crouched down low, ready pounce.

FOUR

"Don't run! Start shouting!" A mysterious voice echoed across the clearing. Without taking their eyes off of the lion, Gabe and Riley decided to listen and started yelling at the top of their lungs. The lion seemed to be startled, and began to retreat a little bit, but it still stayed in it's hunting position. The kids kept shouting as loud as they could, and then, suddenly, the lion was tackled to the ground.

The kids darted over near a tree and watched as a young man wrestled with the lion. How he had knocked it totally off balance, they didn't know. But they watched as the lion pawed at the man and the man fought back. There were roars and shouts from the tangle on the ground, but pretty soon Riley and Gabe could tell that the lion was obviously losing the battle. The young man untangled himself from the lion and started yelling at it to go.

He then pulled out a slingshot, no, *the* slingshot, and started firing rocks right at the lion's head. That was enough for the beast, and he ran off into the valley, never to be seen again.

Gabe and Riley both felt stuck to the ground, amazed at what they had just witnessed and still recovering from the fear. That stranger had SAVED them. A total stranger! And one who had the slingshot!

The young man tucked the slingshot in his belt, shook out his hair, and jogged over towards the kids. "Are you guys alright?"

The two were surprised to see that the man was actually a teenage boy, not much taller than Gabe. He had curly auburn hair and his skin was tanned from the sun. He was thin, but muscular, and wore a tunic just like theirs, but his garments were brown.

"I...I think so," Gabe managed to respond.

"What are you guys doing out here in the open anyways?" Asked the boy. "Kids like you shouldn't be on your own in the valleys."

Riley gulped. "We're just lost," she said, "we were, um, we were…"

"Separated," Gabe interjected, "We were separated from our family on the way home. And they live that way." Gabe pointed out in the opposite direction that the stranger came from.

The stranger nodded and panted, out of breath. "Well, let me help you," he said, "I'll help get you home."

"First," said Riley, "we should probably get you some water. You look EXHAUSTED."

The stranger laughed. "You're probably right. Follow me," he said, "Martha is just over by those trees."

The three walked over to a cluster of trees where a donkey and carriage stood hiding in between them. The stranger pulled a jug from his cart and began to drink in big gulps.

"Thank you," said Riley, "for saving us back there. We owe you our lives!" Gabe and Riley sat down on the grass across from the cart.

"Oh," said the stranger, "it's nothing I haven't done before. I take care of my father's sheep and have to deal with wild animals all the time. I'm just glad this one didn't get a good scratch on me!" He took another big gulp of water. "I'm David, by the way."

"David? Like *the* David?" Gabe nudged Riley in the ribs hard.

"She means that in a good way."

David laughed. "Well, I am the only David in Bethlehem, so I guess I am *the* David. Now, what are your names?"

"I'm Gabe, and this is Riley."

"Well, Gabe and Riley, why don't we get you home, alright? There's just one thing I have to do first. See, my brothers are fighting the Philistines right now, and I have to drop off some supplies. Is it okay if we make a stop there?" The two kids nodded in agreement. David stood up. "Well, let's go, then. We should reach the Israelite camp in the afternoon." He helped Gabe and Riley to their feet, and the trio began the journey to the camp.

"So," Riley asked as they walked, "who in your family is fighting again?"

"My three oldest brothers," said the boy, "they're the strongest so they get to go fight. My father, Jesse, sent me to bring some bread and grain. Martha is just here to help me carry it all." He patted the donkey on the neck.

"How long have they been gone?" Riley continued.

"It feels like forever," David sighed, "I've just been at home taking care of the sheep. Don't get me wrong, I love those little lambs and would do anything to protect them, but still, sometimes you just need a change of scenery to make the days go faster. At least we get our Sabbath day and our rest as a change of pace."

"I like Sundays because that's when we go to chu--" Gabe shot Riley a dirty look, "--I mean temple. We go to the temple."

"I like going there, too," said David, "it's so comforting to know God resides among His people isn't it?" The two children nodded in agreement. "It's also nice to spend time in His word. Always remember that God's word guides you if you stay in it, understand?" Riley and Gabe nodded before continuing the rest of their journey.

At one point they came to a stop so David could feed Martha the donkey and let her drink some water from the creek. Gabe pulled Riley to the side. "We have to stay close," he whispered. "We have to get that slingshot!"

"I know, said Riley? But it has to be *delivered* remember? We can't just grab it!"

"Well, it can't hurt to try. Maybe *time* is the deliverer. Just, try to grab it when you can."

Riley agreed with Gabe's plan, both of them making a pinky promise to try their best. They rejoined David, who was finishing hitching the wagon to Martha, and set off once again. They walked for hours up and over hills and around sharp corners, the path winding all around them, until finally they reached the top of the largest hill yet.

FIVE

"That, my new friends, is the Valley of Elah." Riley and Gabe looked down at the deep valley. Near them, just over to the left were hundreds if not thousands of large brown tents. To the right, what seemed like a mile away stood red tents. "Those are the Philistines over there," said David, pointing to the red tents. "They are vile and cruel and do not serve the God of our fathers. There God is just an idol, a statue of a being named 'Dagon'. It makes me sad, that they are missing out on the blessings of the Lord."

David pointed to the brown tents. "Those down there are the Israelite tents. Remember that there are a lot of people, so make sure that you stay close to me."

The trio walked down the base of the hill to the edge of the camp, where David talked to a guard and quickly set up a small tent. While he was finishing laying out bedrolls for the three of them inside, there came a great shout from the camp around them. David rushed out of the tent. "Come! Hurry and stay close! They are going into battle."

David quickly grabbed Riley's hand, who in turn grabbed Gabe's, and they began to wind through the sea of tents, campfires, and people bustling around. From all sides of them, soldiers in heavy and shiny armor began forming a single file line that wove around the camp.

Gabe looked over his shoulder across the valley and saw the Philistines doing the same thing and filing out onto the field in straight rows. He gulped, taking in the size of the Philistine's massive army. Riley struggled to keep a grip on David's hand as they ran throughout the camp. She didn't even have time to notice all the formations that the soldiers were taking. She just didn't want to get lost.

She could tell David was looking for someone, or anyone he knew. He kept examining the faces of the soldiers passing by him. After a few minutes of running, they finally came to a rapid halt next to a particularly muscular group of soldiers. Gabe and Riley literally fit inside one of the men's shadows because he was so huge.

"Eliab! Abinadab! Shammah!" exclaimed David. "Brothers, what's happening?" Gabe, Riley, and David fell into step with the three brothers, who acknowledged David's voice with a smile, but kept their eyes straight ahead.

"It's time to fight, but today is not the first day we have gone into the valley like this," said one of the brothers, "it's been forty days and not a single fight has occurred."

"Yes," said the brother behind him, "Abinadab is right. We go out and stand, but that is all we have accomplished, other than being afraid."

"But why Shammah?" Asked David, "Why are all of you afra--"

"WHY HAVE YOU COME OUT TO DRAW UP FOR BATTLE?" They had made it to the open section of the valley. As the lines of Israelite soldiers came to a halt, the three friends turned around and saw, in the middle of the valley, someone that could only be described as a giant.

The giant was as tall as a full-grown elephant. His bronze helmet shone in the sunlight-just like his armor. His spear was taller than he was, with a huge, pointed, sharp stone at the top. He had a sword on his hip and an evil grin on his face. The only other person in the middle of the field carried a gigantic and sturdy shield. David moved Riley and Gabe protectively behind his back.

"His name is Goliath, "whispered Abinadab, "Goliath of Gath."

"AM I NOT A PHILISTINE? AND ARE YOU NOT SERVANTS OF SAUL? CHOOSE A MAN FOR YOURSELVES," Goliath roared, "AND LET HIM COME DOWN TO KILL ME, THEN WE WILL BE YOUR

SERVANTS. BUT IF **I** PREVAIL, THEN YOU SHALL BE **OUR** SERVANTS AND SERVE US!" All of the Philistines cheered while the Israelite army shifted around, all of them very afraid to face the giant. "I DEFY THE RANKS OF ISRAEL THIS DAY! GIVE ME A MAN THAT WE MAY FIGHT TOGETHER!" The Philistines cheered again from across the valley, this time banging their shields, the noise thundering between the surrounding hills.

Then, slowly but all at once, the Israelites turned away and retreated, each of them admitting that they did not want to face the giant. Some of the soldiers began running, the terror clear on their faces. Riley quickly followed David's brothers, not wanting to be the last ones left on the field. When they reached the edge of the camp, they turned around to see David slowly walking back, not in a rush at all.

Shammah stooped down next to Gabe and pointed at Goliath. "Do you see that man who has come up?" Gabe nodded. "Surely he has come up to defy Israel. And the king will make the man who kills him rich. He will give him great riches, his daughter to marry, and he will give freedom to his family."

"What shall be done for the man who kills this Philistine and takes away Israel's reproach?" David had finally joined the line of the camp where his brothers, Riley, and Gabe stood. "Who *is* this Philistine? Who is he to defy the armies of the living God?" David's face was angry, upset that all the men in the army were letting Goliath defy them and God.

Abinadab stood up and repeated to David what he had told Gabe, and his angry face was replaced with a thoughtful one.

"David, why have you come down?" This time, it was the brother Eliab that spoke. He was big, bearded, and very obviously annoyed. Riley thought that he looked like a manly version of Reese whenever she found Riley eavesdropping. "Who did you leave the sheep with? I know the evil in your heart, David, and you've come down to see the battle!"

David shot a frustrated look at Eliab. "What have I done now? Was it not just a word?" He turned to Riley and Gabe. "Come now, let's leave Eliab and my other brothers with some peace and we'll turn in for the night."

Gabe and Riley turned and followed David, Riley giving a halfhearted wave over her shoulder.

"Oh," said David, "my siblings can make me so upset! But sometimes, it's better to walk away than to argue."

"I understand," laughed Riley, "my sister drives me CRAZY. All she cares about is her silly boyfriend."

David looked at Riley kindly and placed a hand on her shoulder. "Oh, Riley," he said, "sometimes people think that their world is the only world, just like Eliab thinks this camp and this battle are his world. But do you know who's world it is, really?"

"God's?" She responded, doubting her answer.

David nodded. "Yes, God's. He'll help you through all your disputes. Even the ones with my brothers or the ones with your sister. He's there."

Riley smiled to herself and the trio finally made their way to the tent.

The three climbed inside and each found a bedroll. "Now, come morning I know God will win," said David. "Be sure to pray for Israel tonight, friends. And good night."

SIX

"David?! David, son of Jesse?!" Riley was jolted awake at the sound of David's name being yelled all around the camp. She looked around to see David and Gabe had empty bedrolls and hurried outside. There stood the two boys, waiting for the shouting to get closer. The slingshot was still in David's belt. Riley could almost reach it, her fingers touched the leather, but then--

"I am David!" He stepped forward as a carriage holding a man in very fancy clothes came around the corner.

"Very well," said the man, "I'm here to take you to King Saul of Israel. He requests your presence at once." Riley and Gabe gasped. The *king?!*

"I will go," said David, "but I must bring these two with me. They are under my watch."

"Very well," nodded the man, "climb aboard. I'll take you to his tent." The three friends climbed into the carriage.

"Saul heard about what you said yesterday to your brothers and your friends," said the man, "he thinks your bravery is something to be admired."

"The Lord is my salvation, so why should I be afraid?" David replied.

The man nodded, taking in David's wise words. "I understand you and the King have already met?"

"Yes sir," replied David, "I've played the harp for him for a while."

"That's so cool," Gabe said.

"Actually," said David, not understanding what Gabe meant, "the palace is actually pretty warm in the summertime. I'm sure his tent is just as nice."

Within a few minutes, the carriage had made it to Saul's tent. It was right in the middle of the camp, and it was definitely the largest. They followed King Saul's messenger inside to where a large throne sat. And there sat King Saul.

King Saul was dark and tall–so tall his head nearly touched the ceiling. His eyes were brown and deep, and they looked worried. His brown hair fell to his shoulders and his beard cradled his chin. His bronze armor and thick black sandals looked sparkling new, and the crown on his head looked big enough for Riley to fit around her waist.

"Hello again, David," said King Saul as David bowed. Gabe and Riley bowed, too, following David's lead. "And hello, friends of David." Saul looked at them with his big eyes. "You are very blessed to be in the hands of such a good young man." He turned his attention back to David. "Now, my boy. I'm sure my messenger has told you that I have heard your brave words. Do you not fear Goliath, Giant of Gath? None of my soldiers, not even the best ones, will fight him."

"Let no man's heart fail because of Goliath," said David. "Your servant will go and fight this Philistine."

Saul let out a booming laugh. "HA! You are not able to go against this Philistine to fight with him! For you are but a youth, and he has been a man of war from his youth."

David straightened up a bit, more resolute than ever. "Your servant used to keep sheep for his father. And when there came a lion, or a bear, and took a lamb from the flock, I went after him and struck him and delivered it out of his mouth. And if he arose against me, I caught him by his beard and struck him and killed him. Your servant has struck down both lions and bears, and this Philistine shall be like one of them, for he has defied the armies of the living God. The Lord who delivered me from the paw of the lion and from the paw of the bear will deliver me from the hand of this Philistine."

"It's true, Your Majesty," said Gabe abruptly, "he saved us on the road to this camp from the biggest lion I've ever seen." Riley nodded quickly in agreement.

Saul inclined his head to Gabe in acknowledgment and Gabe seemed to sweep with pride that the king gave him attention. The King paused and thought for a moment. "Alright, go. And the Lord be with you! But first, we must get you in armor to fight."

At once three servants came rushing in, forcing Gabe and Riley over to the side of the tent. One servant put a bronze helmet over David's head, which fell in front of his eyes so he couldn't see. Another brought him armor made out of chains, which caused David to trip when it was put on his shoulders. The last servant brought a sword that David strapped to his side. The armor seemed to swallow David whole and make him look tinier than he already was. He tried to take a step, but lost his balance, swaying in the armor. Riley let out a little giggle before clapping a hand over her mouth.

"Girl," said King Saul, "Why do you laugh?"

Riley felt her cheeks flush red. "I'm sorry, Your Majesty," she said quietly, "it's just, he can't fight with armor that doesn't fit him."

"She's right," said David, struggling while taking off the armor and sword. "I cannot go with these, for I have not tested them. Assemble your soldiers, and I will prepare myself. Thank you for your kindness." David bowed, which caused Gabe and Riley to do so as well, before the three left the tent of the king.

"David!" Gabe called as the two sped up to catch up with him. "What can we do? How can we help?" They approached a small creek running through the middle of camp.

"Please," said Daivd, "help me look for the smoothest stones you can find. That would be a great help."

The three of them spent several minutes combing through the rocks that were in the creek. They came up with about twenty stones, and from out of those David chose five that would fit in the little pouch on his side. Then, the friends turned around towards the valley and the shouting armies that were, once again, lining up there.

SEVEN

"Do you remember where Abinadab was standing?" David asked. The children nodded. "Go stand with him. I will go fight the giant." Even though the children knew how this story ended, they both began to feel very afraid. Riley felt tears beginning to well up in her eyes.

"Oh Riley," said David, wiping the tears that started to fall, "be brave and have faith. And you as well, Gabe." Gabe nodded, standing strong and puffing out his chest a little to show his courage. David then kissed both of them on the forehead before running off into the fray. Gabe and Riley rushed to find Abinadab.

"You two," said Abinadab as they approached, "where's Dav-"

"AM I A DOG THAT YOU COME TO ME WITH STICKS?" Abinadab, Riley, and Gabe looked out and saw a laughing Goliath approaching David with his shield-bearer at his side.

"Oh no," whispered Abinadab.

Gabe and Riley exchanged a worried look. "Have faith," he mouthed to her. She nodded, but, still being afraid, took her friend's hand for comfort.

The Philistine let out a growl that felt like it shook the ground around them. Riley and Gabe could almost hear his big yellow teeth grinding in rage at the Israelites. In front of him stood David, who looked like an ant next to a big oak tree when compared to Goliath.

"COME TO ME," Goliath said, "AND I WILL GIVE YOUR FLESH TO THE BIRDS OF THE AIR AND TO THE BEASTS OF THE FIELD."

Then David said to the Philistine, "You come to me with a sword and with a spear and with a javelin, but I come to you in the name of the Lord of hosts, the God of the armies of Israel, whom you have defied. This day the Lord will deliver you into my hand," the Israelites cheered, "and I will strike you down and cut off your head, that all the earth may know that there is a God in Israel, and that all this assembly may know that the Lord saves not with sword and spear. For the battle is the Lord's, and he will give you into our hand."

Without warning, the Philistine roared like thunder and began to move like lightning. He moved in great strides towards David and began to draw his arm back to launch his spear. Just as quickly, David stepped forward and loaded his slingshot with a single smooth stone. Abinadab quickly covered Riley's eyes by tucking her into his side, but Gabe watched as David released that one smooth stone...it went higher and higher until….

THUNK. It hit Goliath right in the middle of his forehead. Goliath came to a fast stop, his eyes wide with shock. Slowly he dropped his spear and wobbled a bit before falling to the ground face first, dust flying all around him.

EIGHT

Everyone stood in silence, mouths open. You could feel the shock in the air as all of the stunned soldiers, both Philistine and Israelite, stared at the fallen giant, defeated by the young shepherd boy...

"For the Lord God of Israel!" This cry rose from a soldier in the middle of the army, and soon the other soldiers joined in the cheer.

Abinadab quickly set Gabe and Riley on a nearby boulder, just above the heads of the troops, before joining the Israelites in a massive charge toward the Philistines. The Philistines, now that their champion had fallen, ran away as fast as they could from the hundreds of soldiers running their way. The victory belonged to God and Israel.

When the valley cleared, David left the side of Goliath and jogged over to where the two were sitting. They jumped off the boulder and Riley launched into David's arms.

"You did it! You really did it, David!!" Riley shouted.

David laughed and hugged Riley tightly, spinning her around in a circle. "No," he said, setting her down, "that victory belonged to God. Another thing to always remember." He reached out and shook Gabe's hand. "With faith, God works wonders, doesn't he?" Gabe nodded, a huge smile beaming across his face.

David's eyes drifted over their shoulders. "But, my dear friends, I'm afraid our time together is drawing to a close." The kids turned around and saw King Saul standing near the camp's edge, waving David over to him. "I have a friend, Menah, who lives one mile down the road in the direction we were going. He's a very good and just man. Follow the path to his house, and he'll help you rejoin your family."

The two kids nodded, and Riley began to tear up, not ready to say goodbye. David took notice and knelt down in front of her, reaching for his belt.

"Before we part, Riley, I want you to have these." David took the small pouch containing the four unused stones and placed it in her open hand. "Take these and remember that the Lord can do a lot with a little.

"And you, Gabe, take my slingshot." Gabe looked in wonder at the rugged, worn down leather. "Because with faith, Gabe, you have your greatest weapon against any foe."

David kissed both of them on the cheek. "Good luck on the rest of your journey. Remember, it's one mile to Menah's house, and he *will* help. And take care, both of you. God guide you." With that David turned and walked away, stopping by Saul and looking back to give one final wave goodbye before following him into the camp.

That's when Riley and Gabe began to feel the wind pick up around them. "Riley! We did it! David delivered Israel, and he delivered the slingshot to us!"

"We did it!" Riley shouted back, light starting to shine around them and the roar getting louder. "Now we can go home!" They grabbed on to each other's hands one more time and closed their eyes tightly. When they opened them again, they were home.

NINE

Gabe carefully set the slingshot back in the box just how they had found it and replaced the lid. They were both very relieved to be back in their normal clothes.

"I'll meet you back outside," said Riley. They both snuck out of the office, careful to shut the door behind them. The sun was still just starting to set in the sky–it was like no time had passed at all.

Outside, Riley met Gabe with a large pink jewelry box. "My mom gave me this for Christmas," said Riley, setting it down between them in the grass, "but Reese is definitely the one who likes jewelry! It hasn't had a use for me until now." She knelt down and opened the box. At the same time, she reached into her pocket and pulled out David's pouch of rocks. Riley put the pouch inside and closed the box, locking it with a key that she had on a necklace. "There," she said, "now we know they are somewhere safe." Riley put the box back in her room, making sure it was in a safe hiding spot before coming back outside, key necklace secure around her neck.

"Let's both promise that this stays between us," said Gabe, holding out his pinky. Gabe interlocked his pinky with Riley's.

"Yeah, my dad would go crazy if he knew we snuck into his office! And then he'd think that *we* had gone insane if we told him what happened!"

"I wish that we could've stayed in touch with David somehow," said Riley, "he was such a nice guy."

Gabe laughed. "You know we can just read what he has to say, right? It's like he left behind letters for us in the Bible."

"You're right!" Riley beamed, "He did write in the Bible! That's so cool–it'll be like he never left!"

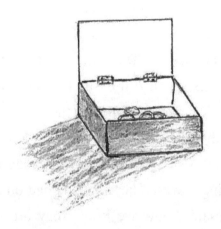

"If this happens to us again, which if your dad brings home more artifacts to be examined, it's definitely a possibility, we may even see him again. Who knows?" They both sat in silence for a moment, lost in thought.

"How do you think all of that happened?" Gabe asked.

"I don't know," said Riley, "but I agree. I do think it can happen again. We'll just have to wait for my dad's next expedition. I think I heard him tell my mom that his dream location is a place called Babylon, but we'll see!"

"Well, hopefully, he finds something," said Gabe. He paused. "Do you think the artifact expert would believe us if we told him it was for real?" Gabe wondered out loud.

Riley just laughed and shook her head *no*. "Come on," she said, kicking the soccer ball towards him, "We still have time for another round of soccer. And I think I'm ready to take down my Goliath."

DISCUSSION QUESTIONS

Use these questions with your children for comprehension, thought, and conversation! These questions are perfect for a small group setting as well.

1. If you could go back to any Bible story, which would you choose and why?
2. David was very brave in facing Goliath. What would you do if you came face to face with the giant? What weapons would you choose? How would you react?
3. Has there ever been a time where you felt small compared to a challenge? How did you face it?
4. What advice would you give Riley and Gabe for their next adventure?
5. David reminded the children that "they can do a lot with a little." What do you think that means?
6. What are some ways you can show your faith daily, even if it is in a small way?

ACKNOWLEDGMENTS

This book wouldn't have been possible without the help of a good family and great friends. To Kitty, Sue, Tammy, Brandon, Carolyn, and Terran: without your helpful edits and wise words this dream of mine would not be a reality. Riley and Gabe's story is like my child and it really took a village to raise it up.

First, to Carolyn Dye. Without your beautiful pictures and hard work, this book wouldn't be half of what it was. You are such an encouragement and such a blessing.

To my parents, who always encouraged my dreams and lifted me up when I could've given up: your support is everything to me and I'd be lost without it.

Nana and Papaws are often overlooked, but I'd like to mention mine. They've always instilled a love for God in my heart, and for leading me to Him I am eternally grateful.

Katie, Matthew, and Sarah, also known as the best cheerleaders ever, you guys are awesome.

Some of David and Goliath's dialogue comes from the Bible, and being able to incorporate it into this work is a blessing.

And finally, this whole book is a love story to the best book ever written. God is at the heart of this book, and I pray that everyone who reads this will come to follow Him and His word.

CPSIA information can be obtained
at www.ICGtesting.com
Printed in the USA
LVHW090435031120
670550LV00004B/277

9 781489 731210